This book belongs to:

....

....

For Clare, Caius & Emily

Quarto is the authority on a wide range of topics.

Quarto educates, entertains and enriches the lives of
our readers—enthusiasts and lovers of hands-on living.

www.quartoknows.com

Publisher: Maxime Boucknooghe
Editorial Director: Victoria Garrard
Art Director: Miranda Snow
Designer: Victoria Kimonidou

Copyright © QED Publishing 2016
First published in the UK in 2016 by QED Publishing

Part of The Quarto Group
The Old Brewery
6 Blundell Street
London N7 9BH

A catalogue record for this book is available from
the British Library.

ISBN 978 1 78493 531 3

Printed in China

There's Only One
Scruffle

Robert Dunn

Ellie loved Scruffle.
He was her bear, and that was that.

Ellie and Scruffle did everything together.

In fact, they were **inseparable.**

Ellie's mum and dad didn't understand why she loved Scruffle so much.

He only had one eye, was held together with mouldy old thread...

...and had a very curious smell.

He smelt a bit like stale cheese
and old socks. **Yuck!**

Ellie's mum decided that she should have a new bear – one with two eyes, clean thread and that smelled of strawberries.

Ellie didn't like the new bear. He smelled **wrong!**

"Can I keep him in the bin?" Ellie asked.

"No, you most certainly cannot!" replied Mum.

"You could try playing with him, for a little while at least," Mum said.

"You won't know what he's really like until you've spent a little time together."

So Ellie thought about it, then decided
to have a walk and think about it some more.

She thought about it while she
played cowboys with Teabag.

Thump!

Thump!

Thump!

She thought about it while she

helped Grandad in the garden...

...and she thought about it while
she painted a picture for Scruffle.

Ellie eventually decided that she would play with the new bear. However, he didn't smell quite as fresh as he had in the morning.

In fact, he smelled **DISGUSTING!**

"Well, I couldn't possibly play with him now!" said Ellie, triumphant.

"Why do you love
Scruffle so much?"
Mum sighed.

Ellie handed Scruffle to her mum. "Well you
won't know what he's really like until you've
spent a little time together, will you?" she smiled.

Ellie's mum suddenly noticed how
soft and cuddly Scruffle was,
if you ignored the smell!

Ellie knew her mum finally understood.
Scruffle was Ellie's bear and that was enough for Mum.

"Can I keep Scruffle and the new bear?" Ellie asked.

"Of course," said Mum,
"but after they've both
had a spin in the
washing machine!"

Next Steps

Ask the children if they have a favourite teddy like Scruffle. Ask them to draw a picture of their teddy, or a toy they would like to have.

Ellie's mum thought Scruffle was too old and smelly to be Ellie's toy. When she gave him a cuddle however, she discovered that he was lovely and soft. Have the children ever been in a similar situation? Perhaps there was a type of food they didn't want to try, which turned out to be quite nice.

What was it about the new bear that Ellie didn't like? Have the children ever been given a toy that they didn't want? How did they react?

At the end of the story, Ellie decided to keep both bears. Why do the children think Ellie changed her mind about the new bear? Ask the children to come up with a name for the new bear. Do the children give their own toys names?

Ellie and Scruffle have lots of exciting adventures together. What do the children think their next adventure will be? Ask the children to come up with some ideas for a story starring Ellie, Scruffle and the new bear.

Ellie has a pet dog named Teabag. Do the children have any pets? What are the names of their pets. If not, what pet would they like to have?